The ADVENTURES ~OF~ ARCHIE

...The Goldendoodle Who Learns A Lot

Written by Betsy Cooper and Marjorie Julian
Illustrated by Kezzia Crossley

This book is for all those children who own a dog or dream of having one.

Archie is a real dog who lives with his owner Betsy.

If he could talk, this might be the way he would describe his life and some of his adventures.

Hi! My name is Archie.
I am a Goldendoodle puppy.

This is the story of my very first adventure.

When dogs have babies, they are called puppies. There are usually lots of puppies born at the same time, and that is called a litter.

My mom is a beautiful Golden Retriever named Penny. My dad is a handsome Poodle named Duke.

I didn't have to wait very long for her to make up her mind. Yay! I was going to live with her and she would take care of me like a mom.

When I was big enough to live with people, Betsy came to take me to my new home.

Our home!

Betsy lives in the city of Vancouver, so we had to travel. I was a bit worried. I didn't know where Vancouver was and I had never been in a big city!

Betsy knew I was scared, so she was really nice and told me we were going to have a wonderful time together. That made me feel a little better.

First, we got on a ferry boat to get across the water.

Have you ever been on a boat like this?

They are really big!

There are lots of cars and people.

Next, we went in Betsy's car to drive to my new home. At first I didn't really like riding in a car. It made my tummy feel funny.

I did have a warm, fuzzy blanket to sleep on though, and pretty soon I fell asleep. Puppies are still babies and they sleep a lot.

When I woke from my nap, we were in Vancouver.

It is beautiful! This would be the perfect place for a puppy like me to grow up. I knew I was really going to like it here.

I saw mountains, the ocean, beaches and lots of parks.

Oh what's this?

We were in a room that moves!

It was an elevator!

Riding in an elevator was fun. The doors opened by themselves and brought us to the 14th floor.

Wow, my new home is up really high and I could see everything.

I saw a park just for dogs and it even had my name on it!

I hoped that I would get to visit that park soon.

When we got to see the apartment, Betsy let me look around all by myself. I found lots of interesting things!

There was a comfy-looking bed for me and it was right beside Betsy's big bed. Maybe I could even jump in with her!

Wow, there were toys and a bone in my own toy box!
There was a ball for playing catch, a rope to chew on,
and even a stuffed animal for me to cuddle.

She must really love me.

Do you have favourite toys? What are they?

You know what?

She was right. When I woke up in the morning, everything was just perfect.

My breakfast was in my own bowl and there were my toys, just waiting for me.

After breakfast we went for a walk.
What was that thing she put around my neck?
Betsy says it is called a collar and a leash and
she put it on so I can't run away and chase squirrels.

She wants me to be safe.

I got to see lots of new things on our walk that day and people even stopped to pet me. I sure do love my new home. This is going to be the perfect place for me to grow up.

I'm really glad that Betsy picked me to be her puppy. I learned a lot on our first adventure. Most of all, I learned that Betsy loved me and would take good care of me. I love her too. :)

...and that is how my life began.

I hope you will enjoy reading about all
of my adventures.

Archie

About the Authors

Betsy Cooper is Archie's owner, Marketing
Communications specialist and former pet store owner
who lives in Vancouver, British Columbia.

Marjorie Julian is Betsy's mother and a retired teacher of
young children. She currently lives in Oakville, Ontario but
spent her teaching career in Kingston, Ontario.

Illustrator

Kezzia Crossley was born in Alberta and currently resides in
Vancouver, British Columbia. Kezzia has an immense passion for
conceptualizing characters and bringing stories to life.
You can see more of her work at www.kezziacrossley.ca

Other books in this series:

Archie Swallows a Ball - publication 2015
Archie Goes to School - coming soon
Archie Gets a Job - coming soon

CPSIA information can be obtained
at www.ICGtesting.com
Printed in the USA
LVHW07n1149061018
592637LV00026B/412/P

* 9 7 8 1 5 0 8 9 7 0 6 3 7 *